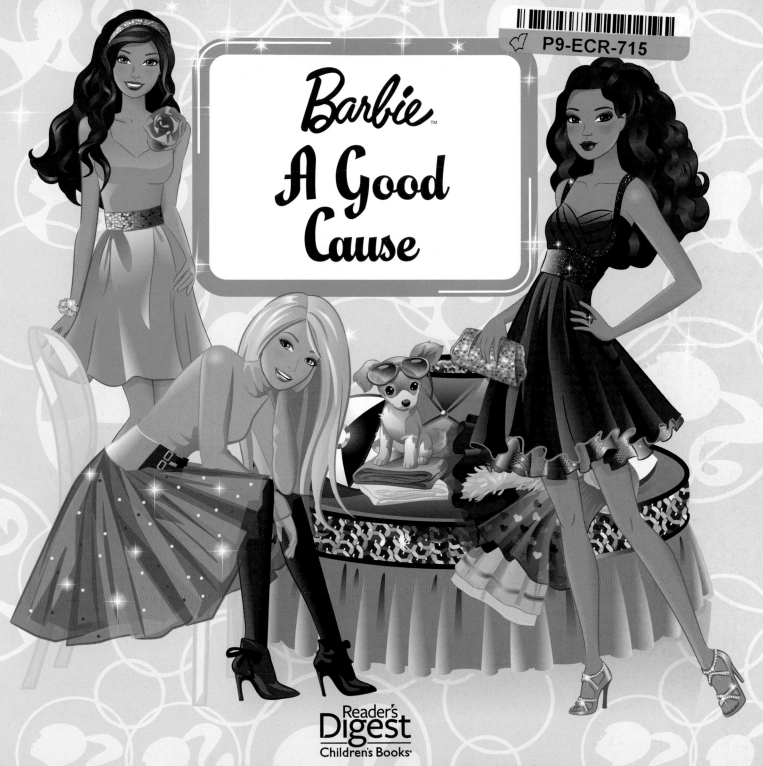

Barbie™
A Good Cause

Reader's Digest
Children's Books®

New York, New York • Montréal, Québec • Bath, United Kingdom

"I'm so glad we're donating some clothes to charity," says Barbie. "I'll finally have some room in my closet."

"It's for a great cause," says Teresa. "The clothes are going to people who really need them."

Teresa and Nikki start sorting through their clothes while Barbie gives her opinion. Even Lacey wants to help!

"Let's try on everything. We want to make sure it all looks good," says Barbie.

"I love your feather skirt," says
Barbie to Teresa.
"Your clutch looks great with
my outfit," says Nikki.
"Hey, I have a great idea,"
says Barbie.

"Even when we wear each other's clothes, we do it in our own way. We should have a fashion show for the charity and show everyone that no matter what you're wearing, you can play with fashion to create your own style," Barbie says.

The girls strut down the runway. Barbie, Nikki, and Teresa each put their own unique spin on their outfits. The audience loves it.

The girls had a great time at the show, *and* helping the charity. And, of course, the newest trend in fashion is to borrow your friend's outfits and style it up your own way. All started by Barbie and her friends! Check out the photos the girls uploaded.

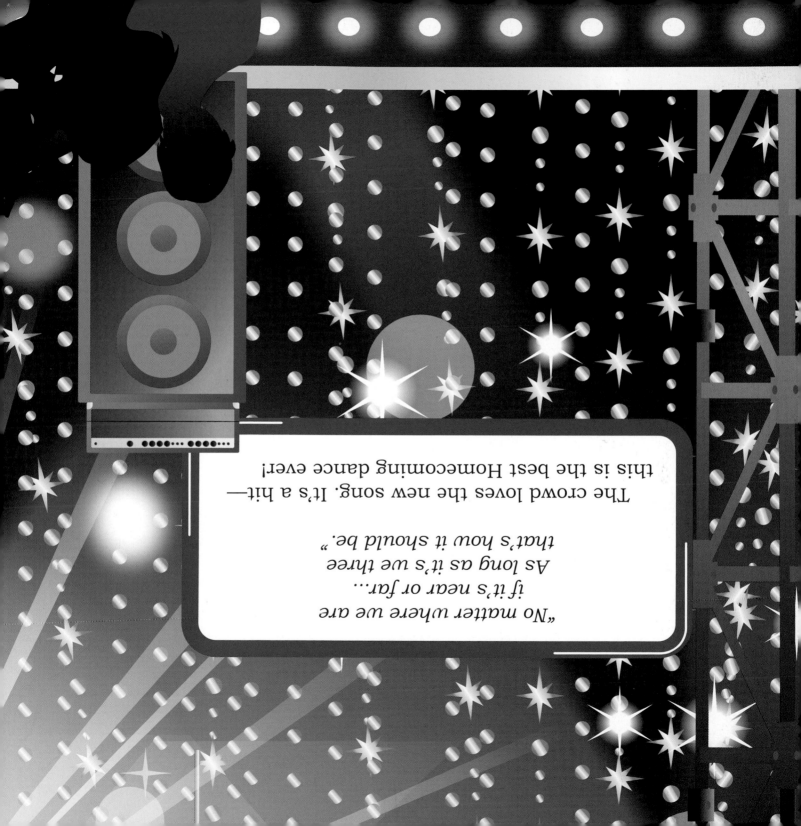

*"No matter where we are
if it's near or far...
As long as it's we three
that's how it should be."*

The crowd loves the new song. It's a hit—this is the best Homecoming dance ever!

"I've got it," says Barbie. "It's not so much where we've been, but that we've been there together! That's what the song should be about—it doesn't matter where you go, as long as you're with your friends."

Nikki and Teresa agree and the song practically writes itself!

"We could write about the places we've been on tour," says Teresa. "The yummy picnic in Paris, that amazing beach in Hawaii...and remember that fair in California?"

But besides that, they're stumped. Oh no... writer's block!

"We have to write a new song for the dance," says Barbie.

"Let's go to lunch and figure it out," says Nikki. The girls jump into Barbie's pink car and head to their favorite café.

Great news! Barbie and her band have been asked to play at the Homecoming dance.

"What do you think, girls? Are we up for it?" asks Barbie.

"Definitely!" answers Nikki.

"We rock!" says Teresa.

New York, New York • Montreal, Québec • Bath, United Kingdom

Reader's Digest
Children's Books®

Barbie™ The New Song